· PREPOSTEROUS ·

EX LIBRIS

· FABLES ·

PREPOSTEROUS FABLES
FOR UNUSUAL CHILDREN

The Tooth Fairy

The Maestro

The Wolf King

The Sorcerer's Last Words

THE
WOLF KING

Written and illustrated
by Judd Palmer

SCHREI WOLF

BAYEUX

Special thanks to the folks who helped to make this book possible:
Shannon Anderson, Ashis Gupta, Dave Lane, Jenny Lane, Jim Palmer,
Marilyn Palmer, Steve Pearce, Anna Asgill-Winter, and Lawren Harris,
whose painting inspired the illustration on page 62.

THE WOLF KING
© 2003 Judd Palmer and Bayeux Arts, Inc.
Published by: Bayeux Arts, Inc., 119 Stratton Crescent SW, Calgary,
Canada T3H 1T7 www.bayeux.com

Cover design by David Lane & Judd Palmer
Typography and book design by David Lane
Edited by Jennifer Mattern

National Library of Canada Cataloguing in Publication
Palmer, Judd, 1972-
      The wolf king / Judd Palmer ; illustrations by the author.
      (Preposterous fables for unusual children)
      ISBN 1-896209-82-3
   I. Title. II. Series: Palmer, Judd, 1972- Preposterous fables
   for unusual children.
PS8581.A555S67 2003   jC813'.6   C2003-905353-9

First Printing: September 2003
Printed in Canada

The Publisher gratefully acknowledges the financial support of the Canada
Council for the Arts, the Alberta Foundation for the Arts, and the Government
of Canada through The Book Publishing Industry Development Program.

to Shannon

Therefore with the same necessity with which the stone falls to the earth, the hungry wolf buries its fangs in the flesh of its prey, without the possibility of the knowledge that it is itself the destroyed as well as the destroyer.

[Schopenhauer: The World as Will and Idea]

Um elfe kommen die Wölfe

Um zwölfe bricht das Gewölbe

At eleven come the wolves

At twelve open the tombs of the dead

[old German counting rhyme]

All the villagers are asleep, except for one.

The Boy Who Cried Wolf

ALL THE VILLAGERS are asleep, except for one.

Everyone else is quietly dreaming under great down blankets, in their warm bedrooms, under snow-covered roofs, under the clear night sky. The peaks and spires of the village glitter blue beneath the cold moon, and the wind blows the spicy smell of pine trees through the empty streets, which softly wheeze with the people's slumber, a hundred chests rising and falling, two hundred lungs filling with air and then emptying, a low rumble of gentle snoring rising through the chimneys, turning to steam and drifting in small clouds of human breath out, over the town walls, and into the black forest.

Grübler the Banker, for instance, sleeps sprawled across his bed cross-ways, as he always does. Every night he wages this war of the mattress with his poor wife, who has once again retreated to the sofa. During the day, Herr Grübler is a tiny man with a tiny voice who makes a tiny impression, but at night he becomes a tyrant, and his dreams are of unfettered power.

Greuel the Mayor sleeps with his toes clenching the blanket. They are long, pale toes, white-knuckled with exertion, for far at the other end of the blanket, where Greuel's head protrudes, his teeth are likewise clamped. Poor Greuel is at war with himself; his teeth pull the blanket up, and his toes down, both with equal determination and equal strength, and in this way his blanket is held in the precise position necessary for nocturnal warmth, despite the fact that his back arches with effort. In his dream, he is a young boy licking the glitter from a cupcake. He will awake with a strange resentment.

Raus the Butcher sleeps heavily and without moving, face-down in his pillow with a puddle of drool collecting in his moustache. He does not dream at all.

Rigid in his bed sleeps Corporal Friedrich Von Kligge of the Town Guard. His uniform is neatly folded on the trunk at the end of his bed. Beside him under the covers, clutched in his austere grip as if he is standing at horizontal attention, is his rifle, bayonet affixed. His jaw is pressed against the oily barrel, pushing his lips into a strange grimace. In his head his dreams are of storm-lashed battlefields, tattered banners, burning forests, and his chest rises and falls to the rumble of tank engines.

On the other side of town sleeps young Eva. She is hidden beneath a mountain of blankets; her nose is the only visible part of her, poking brown and warm out of the profusion of comforters like a small animal emerging from its burrow on a snow-filled plain. Underneath the blankets none can say what her position might be. She dreams of the child in her belly, but she does not yet know the child is there and she will not remember her dreams in the morning.

All the villagers are asleep, except for one.

The one who is awake is a boy, about seventeen years old. He stands on the moonlit wall, watching the stillness of the tree-shadows which cut across the snow like cracks in the earth. Behind him is sleep, before him the sharp darkness of the wood; he is awake amongst the drifting dreams of the village. His own lungs rise and fall with theirs, but he is standing, his eyes open, his neck wrapped in a great wool scarf, his coat too big, the steel barrel of his rifle freezing his fingers through his mittens.

He presses his cheek against the battlement beside him, to stay awake. The cold of the stone is painful. He watches the fog of his breath and feels the frost on his scarf with his lips. His stomach rumbles.

The shadows move. He sees it as though the shadows are fragments of dream, not real, but as the first shaggy shape emerges black against the snow, his blood surges within him, the sleep in him is torn away, and the quiet world is quiet no more.

He panics. "Wolf!" he cries. "Wolf!"

The village stirs. Eyes flicker in the dark. Ears listen. Brains awaken.

"It's just the boy," they think. "Crying Wolf again." And then they go back to sleep, all except Corporal Von Kligge and young Eva, their eyes glinting in their frozen moonlit bedrooms.

The wolves come, like a dark tide, overflowing the walls, pouring into the town's streets, a silent river of teeth and flashing eyes, their paws on the snow like a whispering doom.

The Ravaged World

THE BABY IN YOUNG EVA'S WOMB was named Alfred. Alfred lived happily in that warm place, floating in the darkness, unaware of the terrible devastation wrought by the wolves outside. From inside that quiet paradise, he did not hear the howls and the shrieks, nor see the flashing teeth and shaggy muzzles, the snarling shadows; he did not smell the gunpowder or feel the cling of the night's cold fog. If he noticed the horrors outside at all, it was only as a minor interruption in his slumber, and he merely stretched his little froggish legs and went back to dreaming gentle dreams.

Outside Eva's belly, morning dawned on the village. The sun rose meekly on the dazed towns-folk, who wandered exhausted and blinking through the broken glass, the trampled snow, searching for loved ones amongst the wreckage. A kind of muffled silence lay heavy in the streets, broken occasionally by a wail or a moan or the shouted name of one who was missing.

The wolf attack had been repelled, although barely, thanks to the heroism of Corporal (now Captain) Von Kligge, who, he said, had never trusted the guard on duty that night, and hence had been walking the wall himself. He had therefore been able to make a defense that averted the worst of the assault. He had broken the tide of the wolves' charge, splitting their vanguard, swinging his sabre left and right as the animals flowed past him.

Von Kligge had been found that morning still standing in the middle of a pile of dead wolves. His arms hung limp and exhausted against his sides, his overcoat bloody and torn, his face gaunt, his teeth still bared in a feral snarl like that of his enemies. Around him the snow was melted and stained, and a fetid steam rose from the corpses around him and enshrouded him in a fog much like the cannon-smoke of his dreams.

He was awarded the Wreath of Ash, a woven hat of branches from the Ash tree. The Ash was sacred to the people of the town, since it was known to repel the wolfish kind. The Wreath of Ash was the town's highest honour, and Von Kligge received it with a reluctance both modest and grim, repeating the solemn phrases required of him by tradition whilst kneeling before Greuel the Mayor and the assembled ancients of the town—those who remained, at least.

The former Captain of the Guard, Captain Von Aufstedter, had not survived the attack, and indeed had been entirely surprised as the wolves crashed through his bedroom window. It was not clear whether he had been valiant in his last moments, discovered as he was in his nightgown unarmed beneath his bed, but regardless the Captaincy was now vacant. And so the town bestowed the honour and the special wolf-fur-collared greatcoat (retrieved from poor Von Aufstedter's closet) upon Von Kligge, who clicked his heels, raised his sabre, and pledged his duty.

He addressed the crowd. "As the Captain of the Guard, I proclaim: This catastrophe was caused by deceit. The Boy Who Cried Wolf lied to us twice. We are not to be blamed if we did not believe him the third time. The liar betrayed us and we have suffered as a consequence. We must find the Boy Who Cried Wolf and punish him."

The villagers cheered, glad to have someone to blame, and scampered to take their revenge. Raus the Butcher was hastily deputized Village Executioner, and he ran to his shop to collect his knives.

But the Boy was nowhere to be found. For days they searched the sewers and the basements and the attics of the town, but each new theory uncovered nothing. Eventually, the villagers stopped looking. Raus resigned himself to the butchery of beasts once again, and packed up his new black hood in hopes of another opportunity to wear it.

Clearly, the Boy had escaped into the forest, but the forest was full of vicious wolves, and so the villagers contented themselves with the sure knowledge that he had been eaten. They laughed about it over their beer, bitter, barking laughter, with red faces and strained grins.

The graveyard was amok with fresh mounds, makeshift wooden crosses marking the savaged remains of the good people of the town, while the stone-carver laboured to make proper tombstones. The sheep wandered stupidly through the forest of wooden stakes, foraging for the brown grass that poked through the snow where it had been trampled down to the earth by funeral after funeral.

Young Eva, overwhelmed by a mysterious grief, returned to her bedroom and did not emerge ever again.

But Alfred knew nothing of these events. Inside Eva's belly, he continued to quietly dream, and his dreams were precisely the same as his life awake.

The Birth Of Alfred

THE TIME COMES for all of us when we must forsake our homes in our mothers' wombs, and finally that sad day came for Alfred as well. For all he knew, that warm burrow was the whole of life, but soon its walls began to rumble, and he found himself pushed by unknown forces down a crushing tunnel. Alfred was wild-eyed, struggling, unable to prevent his passage down that inevitable channel. Soon harsh light shone in his blinking eyes as

"It is a Boy," said the great monster that gripped him.

he squeezed his puckered face out of paradise.

In the first moment his little lungs sucked the cold air of the world, he knew he had been thrust into a new and dreadful realm where he did not feel at home. He did not shriek nor wail as is the custom of babies; instead, he silently held on for dear life. But the inexorable heaving propelled him despite his efforts into the doctor's waiting hands.

As the doctor held him aloft, his little chubby red arms and legs struggled in vain to find purchase on something earthbound. But the good doctor held firm, and peered at him.

"It is a Boy," said the great monster that gripped him.

Alfred's first memories were of that gentleman's whiskers, which scratched poor Alfred's brand-new tummy, and the foreign smell of his breath, which was dank and impure to Alfred's unsullied nostrils. The doctor shook him by his legs and stared him in the eye, a trick he had learned, to distract the child as he brought forth the scissors.

And with a snip and a wink, and a quick and efficient swaddling, Alfred was launched into this earthly existence. He would always wish, even as he grew to be a boy, that he could have chosen otherwise. From that day forth, Alfred's life was plagued by misery.

Alfred was the son of the Boy Who Cried Wolf. The people of the village would never trust him; he was born a liar and a liar he would be, for it was in his blood.

The Tormentors

A SNOWBALL FLEW through the air, spinning gracefully, flashing white against the grey sky. With a beautiful eruption of impact, it hit Alfred in the precise spot between his hat and scarf on the back of his head.

A cheer rose behind him. He kept running, staggering through the snow, his thin face red, as another snowball whizzed by him and another sprayed, glancing off his shoulder.

"Bug off!" he cried, panting, but the answer was another gleeful cheer. His adversaries howled as they pursued him, leaping from snowbank to snowbank, their boots crunching a staccato rhythm, clouds of steam huffing from their grinning faces. Alfred's own lurching was no match for the powerful bounding of the three older boys, who cackled and yipped and hurled more snowballs.

Finally, poor Alfred stumbled and fell, plowing a furrow in the snow with his nose. He struggled to turn himself over in time to defend himself against the hurtling arrival of the hunters behind him, but as he twisted to face them they landed, burying him in a pile of knees and elbows and jutting chins.

With Alfred hopelessly pinned beneath them, the Tormentors paused briefly to discuss what to do

"What do you say, ladies, shall we fill its underpants with snow, then?" inquired Grübler, the son of the banker. He fluttered his hands as if he was attending a sinister tea-party.

"No, no, my dear, what if it's hungry?" answered Greuel, the son of the Mayor, affecting an expression of shock. "Perhaps it would like to eat a nice snowball."

"But why not simply bury it? Wouldn't that be delightful?" said Grübler.

"Oh, but what if it cries Wolf? It is a gentle, delicate creature, but it is confused easily. It may cry Wolf, you know," said Greuel.

The two of them looked at Raus, their leader, son of the butcher. The three boys were like one beast with three monstrous heads— they were never seen apart, and indeed might have been better named GrüblerGreuelRaus. They prattled amongst each other constantly in a weird high-pitched whine that they found to be both funny and terrifying. In general, however, their chief joy was causing woe to Alfred, for it is the way of boys, like it is the way of wolves, to cull the pack of its weak.

Raus twirled an imaginary moustache pensively, then brightened with an idea. "First we feed it, then we fill its underpants, then we bury it," he said, and whatever he said was the final word.

And so it came to pass. The Tormentors left Alfred in a heap of snow, clapping each other on the back and tittering as they disappeared down an alley.

Alfred slowly dug himself out of the snow and sighed. It was then that he noticed Martina.

Oh, what a double-pronged moment, what a pair of fangs stabbed Alfred when he saw Martina! The first fang that pierced him was shame, as he stood with underpants bulging with snow, his cheeks tear-stained. But the second fang was more sharp, for it was love.

Yes, poor Alfred was in love with Martina. The sight of her made his heart leap within his

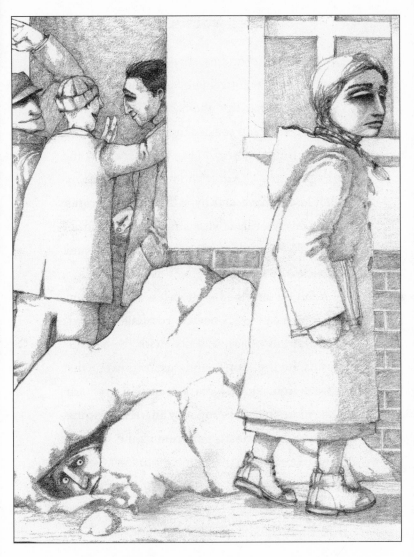

But the second fang was more sharp, for it was love.

little chest, leap and twirl and get entangled in his lungs: her glittering eyes, her noble nose, the curve of her lips, the back of her neck, the way she wore her socks, the whole of her, filled with infinite mystery.

Of course she did not love him back. Why should she love skinny Alfred, whose pants were always filled with snow, whose cheeks were always stained with tears? Why should she love the son of the Boy Who Cried Wolf?

But he imagined nonetheless that he could win her heart with poetry. For fragile Alfred, alone in the village, was alive with the delicate beauty of the world, and his tears were not always from sadness but also sometimes with the unbearable joy brought by an icicle dripping or a shadow against a sunbeam or the smell of pine trees coming through his window.

But in his heart he knew that these things would not entice Martina. No, the only thing that a girl could love in this town was a soldier of the Guard, a man who had proved himself against the wolves with rifle and sword.

For this reason, all Alfred wanted in the world was to join the Guard and walk the walls in defense of the town, to wear the uniform, to show the insignia on his collar. Some day, the wolves would come, and he would cry Wolf and save the village. The curse in his blood would be lifted, his father's lies washed away; he would emerge from the smoke of battle tall and clean, and Martina would come to him with love in her eyes.

He thought about that, as Martina continued on her way down the street, away from him, unaware, perhaps, of the pinioned heart that watched her.

And Alfred, too, continued down the street on his way home.

A Window

THE ENTIRE EPISODE was observed from a window above. It was observed by an old man, old enough to be by and large completely forgotten by the townsfolk. He wore the musty military garments of a bygone age, faded and threadbare, and he was hunched on a gnarled crutch, for he had only one leg. The other had long since been digested by some now long-dead wolf whom he had met in valiant combat many years ago. He watched with a silent melancholy all that transpired outside his window, but seemed to be particularly saddened by the action just described.

The old man was accompanied by another character worthy of note: his dog, also watching through the window, also ancient and wise and sad.

"Oh, poor young girl," said the Old Man. "She does not know the burden she carries."

"And neither does the boy," said the dog.

"The boy does not know the burden he carries?" asked the Old Man.

"He does not know that it is she who carries the burden," answered the dog.

Alfred's Mother

A ND SO, ALFRED ARRIVED at the door-
step to his house. Carefully, quietly, he
opened the door, and crept into the hallway. As
he closed the door behind him the sunlight on
the carpet winked out, and he was again in the
dark and watery domain of his mother.

He did not cry out, "Mama, I'm home."
Instead, he trod softly down the hall in search
of her.

In the kitchen he found the first sign of her

day's activities. On the table was a half-filled cup of cold tea. It was as if, in the shimmering air of the kitchen, he could still see her silhouette: sipping tea and quietly afloat in the strange sorrow that seeped from her always. She haunted the house with tears, and it was by tears the outline of her life could be traced, for on the table was a small lagoon which was not spilled tea.

To the living room, then, trod Alfred, following the glistening waterways of his mother's woe along the floorboards—a drip here, a drip there. But she was not to be seen in her reading chair. Nevertheless, she had been there: the blanket that lay on the chair was damp to the touch.

"To the window," thought Alfred, and up the stairs he sailed, upstream along estuaries and tributaries, past inlets and bays. And there she was, sitting at the window, looking out on the roofs of the town. In the evening's dying

But she was not young again.

sunlight she was ethereal, her delicate fingers resting on her lap, her pale neck long and still. On the window ledge had collected a pool, which had overflowed to run down the wall and gather on the floor around her feet. She turned her lovely face to him, and smiled. Tiny rivers ran down her cheeks, but Alfred did not know why—nor did he wonder, because ever since he had known his mother she had been a creature of air and salt-water, a phantasm whose only palpable presence was that steady trickle.

Had she loved the Boy Who Cried Wolf, and did she weep for love lost? Was that the well of her sorrow?

It was not. She was not in love with the boy who died in the jaws of the forest, and yet still he died loving her. Such are the strange, shadowed paths of the heart: In the watery deeps of her, she knew that if she did love him, then all would have turned out differently. He would be happy beside her now, not torn and wailing in the belly of a wolf somewhere in some cold glade. He would never have needed to lie. When the wind blew from the trees, his moans haunted her even through her locked-tight window.

Even if she did not love him, if she could be young again she would have pretended. But she was not young again; the jaws were shut, and her happiness had long ago been swallowed on that night. It was on that night that she forsook love entirely.

Alfred silently withdrew his handkerchief from his pocket and wiped the wetness from her cheeks. He curled up at her feet then, and she rested her hands on his head.

The house they lived in, it seemed, had an unquenchable thirst for grief. Together they sat for a long while, the snow in Alfred's clothes melting to mingle with his mother's tears to form a great sea.

* * *

On the wall stood Captain Von Kligge, at attention with his rifle. Beyond the wall lay the forest, which glowed red in the sunset, the shadows long and deepening. He was vigilant: His cold eyes peered into the shadows for signs of movement. But in the depths of his soldier's soul, he had other eyes, which stared behind him over the rooftops and chimneys to the very window at which Eva and Alfred sat. The dark parts of himself were always transfixed by that window, which was the only opening into Eva's world, through which it was sometimes possible to see her silhouette, as the day turned to cold night on the wall.

And through that window Eva stared back, watching for the gaunt silhouette of the man she loved but could never have, because the Boy was dead and it was her fault she didn't love him instead.

The Wall

S UNDAY. ALFRED HAD A SECRET.

The wall had been built before anyone
could remember. It was possible that it even
predated the village itself; many great empires
had risen and fallen in this forest, and the
giants of old built many strange structures in
the wood whose purpose had long been forgotten. Perhaps the wall had been the fortifications for an imperial city, from which a gaunt

Tsar had ruled in a bygone age, sending forth his armies to conquer and burn. Or perhaps it had been the last defense of a gentle people against a nomad horde, which came shrieking from the eastern steppes on shaggy horses, firing black feathered arrows and shaking curved cruel blades. Perhaps the wall had held back the onslaught, or perhaps not. Perhaps it had been the walls of a cathedral, or of a garden.

It was hewn from grey stone, carved in great blocks. Strange writings were scratched into its surface—whether they were symbols of arcane power or the graffiti of conquerors or conquered, nobody knew. In more recent years, the additional fortifications of wood or iron had been added to the wall, filling in ancient cracks or adding towers where they were needed. It was now a complicated, ramshackle structure, rising out of the forest floor entangled in weeds and black tendrils of dead ivy. In the winter when the wall was capped by snow it had the look of a wrinkled old man with hoary hair and old battle-scars.

The wall was patrolled at all times by the soldiers of the Guard, who wore thick overcoats and wolf-fur hats, carrying rifles and swords, watching the forest. They could not see far, because the forest was dense and shadowed. They tried to cut down the trees next to the wall, so that they could have some sense of the surrounding country, but the forest always crept back to encircle them again. Beyond their vision the forest stretched to the edge of the world, tangled, dark, alive, impenetrable.

In the forest had always been wolves. They roamed the ragged glooms like spectres, living amongst the huge roots and cold brooks, burrowed in holes in the earth or racing, blood-mad, through the flitting trees. Now and then, the winter would be hard, their antlered prey would be few, and they would turn their red eyes to the village.

In those dark times, the only impediment to their hunger was the wall, and those men on the battlements, and the guns and blades they carried. It was the wall between human and beast, between hearth and the howling world.

But unbeknownst to the village, there was a hole. Amongst the brambles in the oldest part of the wall, the stones were heaped as though they had once been smashed by some siege engine in centuries past; a tall palisade had been built to fill the breach, but in the ruins at the overgrown base there was a route through, too narrow for a wolf, but just big enough for a small boy.

It was Alfred's secret way to escape the sorrows of his life. He crept through it every Sunday, through the dank and icy tunnel, out of the cramped village and into the infinite forest.

He knew there were wolves, but he risked it nonetheless, for he needed to remind himself each week that life was much larger than it could appear, that a hardy soul could roam where it pleased if it was prepared for danger, that he would someday be a wanderer of the world.

And so, it was Sunday, and Alfred set forth on his expedition, with a lump of cheese in his pocket.

The Forest

ALFRED CRAWLED ON HIS BELLY until he had reached the trees, where he would not be seen. Then he stood, and breathed the thick air of the forest. He set off along whichever route pleased him, knowing that if he lost his way he could easily climb a tree and spot the grey wall, in whichever direction it might lie. Regardless, he never went too far, because the twisting branches and tangled roots made it hard going. Mostly, he liked to find a nice tree and sit in it, looking out over the wood and imagining it his own domain.

Sometimes a deer would pass silently below him, or a raven would land on a branch next to him, regard him with black eyes, then flap away on oily wings.

Today he found a great old oak and clambered to the top of it, the sun warming him in the upper golden branches. He sighed contentedly and pulled out his cheese for a nibble. His thoughts drifted with the gentle rustle of the trees in the wind, and the hours floated by as he dreamt of Martina.

He slowly became aware of a strange silence, as if the forest had taken a breath. His leg had fallen asleep, so he shifted his position, and looked about from his perch.

His fingers clenched the branch. Suddenly, the indistinct shadows on the mottled snow below resolved in his vision into fearful shapes: He was surrounded by wolves.

They stood perfectly still, their great ship-keel chests expanding and contracting slowly. Alfred could hear the quiet hiss of their hot breath turning to steam in the frozen air. They stood in a perfect circle amid the roots, their terrible jaws thrust towards him, their eyes unblinking, unmoving, staring at him. It looked as if they had gathered to worship at the revelation of some miracle in the tree, but in a wolf the mystical and the murderous are one thing. Their black noses twitched slightly with the smell of blood in Alfred's veins.

Alfred froze. In all his young life he had never seen something so beautiful or so terrible as those seven wolves arrayed below him, waiting. In each of their eyes he could sense a vast knowledge, older and more cruel than the babble and chatter of the village. In that moment he could hear the storms blow in the darkness before creation, before humans had ever been dreamt, before their stupid feet had ever trod

In a wolf the mystical and the murderous are one thing.

this earth. He trembled.

For hours they regarded each other, boy and wolves. The patience of the wolves was infinite, it seemed, and Alfred's terror kept him gripping the branches with white knuckles until the pain of effort ran through his arms into his aching spine. They could outlast him, he knew.

The sun drifted through the watery sky, slowly past the treetops, the shadows growing longer like fangs in the snow, and still the wolves waited for their prey.

A Man In The Wood

IT WAS MIDNIGHT. The wolf eyes glinted a ghastly yellow, in each black pupil the moon reflected. Alfred shivered in delirium. A thousand times he had felt himself falling through the branches, snapping wood, the crunch of his bones as he landed on the forest floor, and then the hot breath and the teeth. But still he held on, and the wolves waited.

Then: a strange howl in the distance, not quite like something from a wolf-throat, that harrowed Alfred's soul, a howl like the wind rattle-shaking bone branches on a winter night, like the moon's grief or the call of fallen souls from beyond the gates of the world. The wolves twitched, still staring at Alfred, but their ears swiveled towards the horrible wail.

Again the howl, making the trees quiver as it swept through the wood. Closer, now, moving fast.

And then, in the pale glow of the moonlit snow, Alfred saw a man. His silhouette mingled with the shadows to make him enormous and dreadful, a ragged form of shade and nightfog. He was dressed from head to toe in grey tatters, his beard savage, covering his face so that only his long nose and glittering eyes could be seen.

The man looked at Alfred with a chill indifference. Alfred searched the man's face for sympathy, but all he could see was a hot and invincible pride.

He regarded Alfred for a coiled moment,

and then, imperceptibly, his gaze softened to a kind of cruel amusement. He made an almost invisible sign with his hand, and suddenly the wolves were gathered around him.

The man laughed, a hollow, strange laugh like a growl, and then turned and was gone, the wolves with him.

Alfred's strength gave out, and he slithered from his branch, twigs snapping and lashing as he fell to the snowy ground. He lay amongst the paw prints for a long while, the wild lingering wolf-odour thick in the air, before he could will his battered body to stand and then to run back to his secret hole in the village wall.

Soon he was in bed with his covers over his head and the moon coming through the window.

Alfred's Birthday

ALFRED COMBED HIS HAIR carefully and straightened his jacket. Today, he was fifteen, and he was now old enough to join the Guard. As was the custom, he would present himself at the barracks, to pledge his allegiance to the wolf-fur-collared Captain. He would receive his sword and his rifle and his greatcoat with the insignia of honour.

He marched down the street to the barracks with a straight back and a thin-lipped expression he thought both noble and deadly, for it was the custom of the Guard to always look as if their duties were arduous and grim but shouldered nonetheless for the sake of all.

When he arrived at the iron door to the Captain's quarters, Grübler, Greuel, and Raus were lounging in their uniforms, leaning on their rifles, their scabbards under their great-coats, their fur hats cocked impertinently on their heads. They grinned as Alfred approached, and Alfred suddenly felt as skinny and small as he actually was.

"How dear! It thinks it's a man," said Grübler.

"It brings a tear to my eye, it does, the gentle thing, trying to look brave. Oh, ladies, isn't it the sweetest?" said Greuel.

"I could just die, I really could. To think of that tiny innocent creature on the wall. What if the wolves come? It breaks my heart," said Grübler.

"To think of it, trying to draw its sword!" cried Greuel.

"And the terrible teeth on its throat!"

"I couldn't bear it. Send it back! Don't let it join the Guard!"

Alfred heard all these things as he walked, but he hoped he did not show them how terrified he felt. He had fooled himself with his hair combing and jacket straightening, but in his heart he remembered the wolves and the man in the wood, and he knew that in the end he would not be able to face them again. But then he thought of Martina, imagined her admiration when she saw him in his uniform, and steeled his courage.

Raus stepped in front of him. Grübler and Greuel tittered.

"This is no place for the son of the Boy Who Cried Wolf. Go home," growled Raus.

"It's my right and my duty," said Alfred.

Suddenly, the Tormentors howled and

pounced, snarling, knocking Alfred into the all-too-familiar snow. Grübler and Greuel yipped and barked with glee, holding Alfred's arms, as Raus licked his lips and showed his teeth. "Are you truly ready?" he whispered in Alfred's ear, as he made to close his jaw around Alfred's throat.

Alfred did not shriek. Without knowing what he was doing, his knee jabbed into Raus's belly, and Raus groaned as he fell over. "Wolf," Alfred hissed, as he twisted himself free of the startled Grübler and Greuel, and scrambled as fast as he could toward the door.

He got his fingers on the handle and was turning it when he felt the furious grip of Raus on his leg. With a crazed strength he managed to open the door and heave himself in, flailing and thrashing, and then slam the door shut just as he freed his leg and pulled it through. With an iron clang, he was safe.

Captain Von Kligge

HORRIBLY, ALFRED REALIZED he was on the floor, his jacket torn, panting, in the office of the Captain of the Guard. He tried to still his lungs as he picked himself up and stood at attention.

Captain Von Kligge sat behind his desk like a stone from the very wall he commanded. Behind him on a hook hung his wolf-collared coat with the scarlet insignia, and next to it his sabre and holstered pistol. Banners of the

"Tell me your duty," the Captain said.

Guard platoons hung on flagpoles, old and tattered with honourable battle, the names of the units in gold letters inscribed: Soil and Strength, Blade and Bullet, Honour and Eyes. The rest of the room was filled with the trophies of a hundred hundred years of war on the wolfish kind, stuffed with straw and posed to remind of their evil.

"Reporting for duty, sir," said Alfred.

"Duty?" said Von Kligge, not looking up from his papers.

"Yes, sir," said Alfred.

"Tell me your duty." The Captain glanced briefly at Alfred and in his eyes there was a strange scorn.

"To Stand with Steel, sir."

The Captain shifted some papers and cleared his throat. "You will not be needed," he said, and Alfred choked.

"It is my fifteenth birthday, sir," he managed.

"Nevertheless, you will not be needed," said Von Kligge.

"But the Wall Needs Youth!" cried Alfred, knowing he was overstepping propriety.

Von Kligge stood suddenly, and Alfred shrank from him. Standing amongst the trophies, he reminded Alfred of the man in the wood.

"Listen to me, boy," said Von Kligge. "The fate of this village is held in vital trust by the men who walk this wall. They cannot fail in their duty. I know this all too well, for I have fought the beasts for my whole life, and I have the fang-scars to prove it. Do you doubt my vigilance?"

"Never, sir," stammered Alfred.

"This war has made me strong. The wounds have covered over with harder flesh and there are no holes in me any longer. Likewise my heart, which is now made of iron. To see Evil is easy, but to take action, to draw your sword and strike, that takes a man, not a coward. Which are you, boy? I think you are a coward."

"I am not a coward!"

Von Kligge stared poor Alfred down. "You lie. You are the son of the Boy Who Cried Wolf and you cannot be trusted. Begone."

But this was not the true reason that Von Kligge hated him. Von Kligge hated him because Von Kligge loved Alfred's mother, and Alfred was the son of another man.

And Alfred obeyed, opening the door and succumbing without a word to the Tormentors waiting outside.

"He must measure himself, I suppose," said the dog.

The Old Man
And His Dog

FROM THEIR WINDOW, the Old Man and his dog watched poor Alfred returning home. The Old Man had a thoughtful pull on his pipe.

"A fatherless boy does not know how to measure himself," said the Old Man. "His mother loves him, he knows, but that is a given, so it is not a measure."

"The world is a measure," offered the dog.

"But the world is infinite, and therefore

cannot be the measure for a small boy," said the Old Man, who put down his pipe and rubbed his foot, for his toes were cold.

"He must measure himself, I suppose."

"That is more than a dog should proclaim," said the Old Man. "For a dog knows his measure is his master. A wolf, on the other hand...."

"Yes, you are right," said the dog. "Shall I get your slipper?"

"You are a good dog," said the Old Man, closing the drapes.

Alfred's Father

ALFRED DID NOT TELL his mother what happened, but one night as they sat quietly sipping their broth he asked her a question that had been weighing upon him greatly since that day.

"Why did my father cry Wolf, mother?"

His mother put her spoon down and stared at her bowl. "Nobody knows, Alfred." She was not telling the truth.

"Do you think perhaps he saw the wolves

but they ran away before anybody else saw them?"

"Perhaps," said Eva.

Alfred looked at his reflection in his spoon. His nose was large, and his chin tiny. The spoon made him look much older, as if his face had crumpled and stretched with age. He looked at his mother, who sat quietly on the other side of the table, her hands folded now in her lap. "But is that what happened?" he asked.

His mother was still. "That's probably what happened," she said.

"Then he wasn't lying. He wasn't a liar."

"That's right."

Alfred thought for a moment. In his mind he saw a happy scene: His mother, her eyes dry of tears, sat at her place, and he in his. But there was another bowl on the table, and there sat his father. They laughed about something, and Alfred showed his father his new uniform. His father glowed with pride to see it, and told a great story about his own adventures on the wall, while Alfred listened and felt the warm tingle of anticipation in his belly.

But the table had only two bowls, two chairs, two spoons. Alfred's heart darkened, for he knew he was imagining a ghost. But it was such a happy thought. "What if he wasn't dead, mother?"

His mother rose and stood behind him, with her wet hands on his shoulders. "Ask me no more," she said in his ear, "except to know that I love you more than anything."

Alfred nodded, and sat still. Night fell upon the lonely pair.

Moonlight

THE MOON WAS LARGE outside Alfred's bedroom window, and it made his room bright with a blue glow. The folds of his blanket looked like snow-covered hills and valleys running with cold brooks.

Alfred lay awake in his bed, staring at the ceiling. His heart was hot within him. He could feel it pulsing in his neck and wrists. He was angry.

He cursed the village and he cursed Von

Kligge. He cursed under his breath in the moonlight all the ways in which the world had transpired against him. His father was not a liar. He knew it in his bones.

Finally, he pretended to sleep no longer, and threw the blankets from him. He dressed quickly, and slipped down the stairs and out the door into the street.

The icy air did not cool his heart. He saw his shadow on the pale ground, and it was long as if he was gigantic. Slowly he raised his arms over his head and assumed a position of monstrosity, and his shadow was a terror to behold, if any besides Alfred were there to behold it. But he was alone, and the sleeping people of the village did not know what a furious spectre roamed in that moon-strange night.

Through the streets he prowled, hunched over, snarling quietly to himself. He loped from one window to another, peering into bedrooms, fogging the glass with his wild breath. In his

A furious spectre roamed in that moon-strange night.

mittens he felt his fingers turn into claws. He let his tongue loll in the cold against his fangs.

Soon he found himself creeping through his secret hole and into the forest. He did not care what happened to him as he slithered on his belly along the ground, unseen by the guards. When he reached the trees he leapt to his feet which had become paws and ran with great leaping strides, ducking branches and dodging roots with a perfect grace that surprised him.

As he ran he felt a surging within him. He threw his head back and howled into the night, a long warbling cry, to tell the world that he was not to be trifled with.

His call was answered by a thousand voices, and suddenly Alfred knew he was just a boy again. He staggered to a halt, eyes wide, and wondered where he was.

He stood in a clearing. Around him on all sides the forest was thick with shadow, and he stood stark in the middle of the moonlit field like the pupil of a great white eye. He knew without knowing that he was being watched.

And then, slowly, the forest moved. From the shadows seeped the wolves, a thousand arched backs and ten thousand white teeth, as far as Alfred could see, an ocean of black moving to surround him. He turned in a slow circle and saw there was nowhere to run.

The wolves pressed close upon him, their breath hot on his face. He could not see past them now as he lowered himself to the ground and covered his head desperately, as they brushed against him, jostling, panting, so many claws on the snow that it seemed deafening. Alfred thought of his young life, his dear sad mother, and of Martina, who would never love him, never ever.

The Wolf King

W HAT FOOLISHNESS BRINGS YOU to the forest at night?"

Alfred uncovered his head slowly and looked.

It was the man. He sat astride an enormous wolf, riding it like a horse, staring down at Alfred with that same look of cruel amusement. With a lithe grace he drew his sabre and suddenly the tip was under Alfred's chin, drawing him to his feet. The sword flashed back into the scabbard at the man's waist.

Alfred could not find the answer to the

"I am the Wolf King."

man's question, nor did he know if it was right for him to speak. He felt the cold damp of fear beneath his coat.

"You must be tormented," said the man. "No happy boy comes out here to the wolves."

Alfred found a little of his voice. "Who are you?" he asked. It came out like a whisper.

The man's eyes flashed. "I am the Wolf King."

Alfred wanted very much to be a king. "How did you become king of wolves? Were you born that way?"

"In a way. I was not born a king, but I was born to become one." The Wolf King peered at Alfred. "You do not have the look of a king, nor the smell. But one never knows for certain at your age."

"I am no king," said Alfred.

"Not yet, at any rate. Still, it takes courage to go beyond the wall. Courage and foolishness. Tell me: why are you so foolish?"

"My life is not happy, as you say. I am angry, I think."

The man laughed. "Learn from the wolves, boy. They are never angry nor do they think. To do so they would have to be separate from the world, but they are beings of the same order as trees and soil and sky. Do you dream?"

"Yes," said Alfred. "But my dreams are strange."

"A wolf dreams also, but it understands its dreams with perfect clarity. Only a man finds his dreams confusing. His own nature appears to him as bizarre. He tries to interpret his visions with occult philosophies and superstitions, but in the end the night vanishes in the morning light. It is the same with dogs, by the way, who once were wolves. You might wonder: What were you, before you lost your way?"

"A moment ago I think I dreamt I was a wolf," said Alfred.

"Well, then, I will tell you something," said the man. "It is weak and pitiful to live behind a wall. A wolf has the whole world as his kingdom, but he must be hardened and fierce. Whether you are beast or man, know that it is in your blood and your race is irrevocable. You must only answer when you are summoned."

The Wolf King looked at Alfred for a moment. "I like you, boy. There is some kindred wilderness in you I find promising. Can I trust you?"

"Yes, sir," said Alfred, "of course."

"Then keep quiet. Tell no-one about me. For the moment I prefer to be unrevealed."

"Yes, sir."

"Very well. Tonight I will let you live."

The wolves parted to expose a path. Alfred blinked. "Thank you, your majesty," he said, and bowed.

The man laughed again. "In the end, I may spare you. Now, run!" With that, the Wolf King wheeled on his steed and with a bound he was gone into the trees, leaving Alfred alone with the wolves.

The wolves began to growl in a low and terrible rumble, and Alfred knew that they drooled for him and that only for a moment were they still at bay. So he ran, as the growl turned to a barking and yowling, through the forest as fast as he could. He could feel the spell break behind him and the sudden frenzy as the wolf-horde burst into the chase.

The trees whipped his face as he hurtled through the brush, and the panting and yelping surrounded him on all sides. Alfred ran, his lungs heaving, careening towards the wall. And through the hole he plunged, hitting the stone, scraping, bloody, as the wolf snouts snapped at him, frustrated. Alfred cowered in the dank tunnel.

Then suddenly, from above, the cry.

"Wolf!" Muffled gunfire from the wall. Alfred saw through the crack the wolves disappearing into the trees as if the forest had inhaled a dark breath and then, silence.

HOMO HOMINI LUPUS

THE WOLVES WERE OUTSIDE THE WALL last night," whispered Martina to her friend Renata. Alfred sat behind them at his desk, listening, ignored. It was a study period, and the students were supposed to be reading Latin. Herr Doktor Faulbeit, the aged professor, was napping peacefully at his desk, his moustache fluttering with his snores.

"How do you know?" whispered Renata.

"Raus told me. He was on the wall, and he shot at them. He thinks he got one."

Renata gasped, and Martina blushed.

Alfred tried to swallow but his mouth was dry. This was an opportunity. He leaned forward, his heart pounding, and whispered between them. "He missed," said Alfred. "I was there."

Renata rolled her eyes. "You were not there. You're not allowed on the wall."

Alfred was horrified to learn that the entire school, obviously, knew of his rejection. But he had a retort. "I wasn't on the wall. I was outside it. With the wolves."

Martina turned and looked at him. It was the first time he had ever actually seen her head-on; before he had only caught surreptitious glances out of the corner of his eye. She was far more beautiful from the front than he could have ever imagined. He felt his face turn red, but he tried to look as if he hadn't noticed her at all. It was all he could do to pretend he was only interested in talking to Renata. "I was with them all night. They fear me."

"What an idiot," said Renata. "Who'd believe that?"

Indeed, Alfred had gone too far. He knew it as he said it. But there was no going back. "It's because I'm friends with the Wolf King."

"You're so weird," grimaced Renata, but Alfred saw out of the corner of his eye that Martina was still listening.

"I'm going back out to visit him again. If either of you is brave enough, you can come with me. It's very beautiful outside the wall at night, when the moon is good. It's easy to find your way back if you climb a tree. And you don't have to fear the wolves if you're with me."

"Silencio!" Faulbeit had awoken.

Alfred thought he saw Martina glance back at him before she returned to her textbook. He felt as if he might float to the ceiling, and he could not concentrate on the page in front of him.

Homo homini lupus, his textbook said. *Man to man is a wolf.*

Martina

MARTINA WAS NOT precisely the person Alfred thought she was. To him, she was a shimmering creature only, and he confused the depths of his own heartpain with a depth of understanding.

In truth, she was more poetic of soul than he could ever have hoped. She was enamoured with the smell of sweaters, with the feeling one gets on rainy nights, with the lives of saints. Indeed, when Alfred was pining at the moon outside his window, composing poetry that he hoped to use to woo Martina, she was usually regarding the same moon and writing her own poetry (poetry that was, frankly, much better than Alfred's). The world of wonders that he hoped to reveal to her was already her world, and she needed no knight in shining armour to take her there.

Had Alfred known this, there would have been a much better chance of their union. But he was obsessed with his own loneliness, and the only way he could make himself feel better was to think of himself as the solitary possessor of secret, mystical truths.

Nevertheless, Alfred's declaration about the wolves intrigued Martina. She, too, stared at her textbook while thinking about something else entirely.

The bell rang in the quadrangle, and class was dismissed. She bid adieu to Renata and walked thoughtfully down the hall to collect her coat and scarf.

There were many forces at work that might have prevented Alfred from attempting to speak to her again after class—fear was chief among them. But after Alfred's strange adventures in the forest he found that he had developed a kind of crazed bravery, and so he hastily grabbed his books and followed her to the coatracks.

Bravery does not constitute eloquence, however, and Alfred found himself standing awkwardly next to Martina without any idea of what to say. Luckily, she turned to him, and did not turn away. To Alfred's delight, she stepped close, and whispered to him conspiratorially.

"Do you really go outside the wall at night?" she asked.

"I do," said Alfred, or at least he tried to say it, but in his attempt to whisper he found himself more or less squeaking instead. "Yes, I do," he added, in a more impressive voice.

"How do you get outside without being seen?"

"I know a secret way," said Alfred, unwisely trying to remember a love poem he had rehearsed a thousand times. Alas, he was not thinking about what he was getting himself into.

"Will you show me?" said Martina, for her part also nervous, a fact which would have never dawned on Alfred in a million years.

Alfred tried unsuccessfully to look like he was reluctant to reveal the secret to a stranger. "I guess, if you don't go blabbing about it. I never noticed you before, but now that I'm talking to you, I think you might be different from the others. There is some kindred wilderness in you I find promising." He made a ridiculous show of looking over his shoulder to see if anyone was listening. "Meet me at the school at midnight. Travel light. Don't tell a soul."

Martina nodded, Alfred's heart almost

exploded, and they made a pantomime of 'here-I-am-putting-on-my-coat-and-heading-out-the-door-like-I-do-every-day-as-if-nothing-happened' that might have convinced any onlookers.

But it did not convince Raus, who was strangely distracted from the conversation about farts he was having with Grübler and Greuel down the hall.

Midnight

ALFRED, HIS HAIR COMBED to within an inch of its life, stood under the school gate. He was wishing that he had thought of some dangerous-sounding password for Martina to say, so that he could appear as if otherwise he might not be sure it was her. Of course it was much better that he hadn't, because his love for her was as obvious as the sky, and she was already a little tired of his pretenses as she approached.

The aforementioned sky was unfortunately filled with clouds, which blocked the moon and therefore made the expedition even more absurdly dangerous. It was much darker than a prudent adventurer would accept, but neither Alfred nor Martina was prudent.

Despite all these things, the excitement of their nocturnal rendezvous overwhelmed them both. Alfred almost proclaimed a poem when Martina arrived, she was so very beautiful in her burglar-style outfit, and Martina herself had to admit that Alfred looked kind of dashing in the shadow of the arch, even though his hair looked brutalized and he should have been wearing a hat in the cold.

Alfred had worked out a daring choreography of sign-language to indicate that Martina should follow him, and through the dark streets they crept like assassins.

They wriggled on their bellies through the secret hole into the trees, and Alfred signaled to stand up probably much later than he needed to. He caught his breath, because Martina had a smear of mud on her cheek that made her beauty somehow even more excruciating.

"It's safe to talk now, I'd say," said Alfred, as if he was an expert.

"It's beautiful already," said Martina, looking around her. Indeed it was: The world outside was enormous, and the infinite dark made her tremble wondrously. By 'already' she meant that they could both agree that they had gone far enough without losing face, and that Alfred needn't go about proving his mastery of wolves, but Alfred didn't notice that she had given him an escape route.

"Just wait until you see the wolves," said Alfred. "There's nothing like it, running with them through the trees, knowing there's nothing to fear. Lucky for you you're with me, otherwise an encounter with the wolves might not be so pleasant."

Alfred could not believe he was doing it, but he reached out and offered his hand to Martina.

Martina was shocked. She was the prettiest girl in the school, and she knew which kind of boy could offer his hand to her and which kind could not. Alfred had gone too far.

But the forest was marvellous and frightening, and excitement and trepidation swirled in Martina's heart. She looked at Alfred, bravely offering to lead the way, and a feeling stirred in her. Here was a boy unlike all the others: a boy with courage to go beyond their little village, to plunge into the trees which stood like sentinels encircling her world. Everybody thought Alfred was just the tear-stained son of the Boy Who Cried Wolf, but she knew now that he was wild and full of secrets. She let him take her hand, and his fingers were warm and wonderful to hold. She felt safe and daring all at once, and her breath fluttered.

And Alfred forgot completely about the danger they were in. His little heart pounded as they picked their way through the dark. He was overwhelmed by joy; his miseries seemed far away. All he could think about was that hand in his own, and the world around them passed as if in a blissful dream.

But the dream dissolved all at once, for suddenly they saw the eyes. On all sides, as if they stood in a candlelit cathedral, glowing pinpricks observed them.

And then the howl of the Wolf King came, a long and terrible banshee moan, hurtling through the forest like a gale of ghosts.

"That's the Wolf King," he whispered. "Do you hear him?"

Martina nodded. Almost without knowing it, they were hugging each other. Alfred felt a glorious courage surge in him, with his arms around his true love, protecting her against the wild winter world. He had never felt so grand,

"The Wolf King is coming," Alfred said.

so powerful, as he did in that moment.

"The Wolf King is coming," Alfred said. "But don't worry. We're safe. You'll see. He's my friend."

The eyes got closer in the darkness until they realized that the wolves were right next to them. Alfred became aware of the churning of his stomach, and that he was shivering in fear. He hoped Martina did not notice. She did.

A muzzle brushed Martina's arm, sniffing, and she cursed the ways of proud boys and curious girls.

"Were you lying about the wolves, Alfred? You should tell me," she whispered.

"No," said Alfred, offended. "I'm not a liar."

The Liar

THE VOICE OF THE WOLF KING came from the gloom, like a gust of winter wind. "What have you done, boy?"

"Greetings, your majesty," said Alfred. "It is me, Alfred. I have brought a guest tonight. She is a girl."

"I can see that. It is you who cannot see in the dark." His voice was cruel. "You are helpless. This is my domain. This is my army. And I cannot allow children to prowl in my kingdom."

Alfred felt a twist in his guts. "I'm sorry," he said. Martina looked at him in terror, for it was beginning to be perfectly clear that she had made a great mistake in following this boy into the forest.

"Your apology is nothing to me. And it will not save you."

In the darkness they heard the slither of a sword coming from its sheath. A low growl grew around them, and the shadows rustled, panting, teeth like an army of pale spectres reflecting in the gloom.

Martina and Alfred froze. Between them they felt the heat of the Wolf King's breath, smelt the wild forest stench of him.

The Wolf King snarled into Alfred's ear. "I have let you live twice. That was very generous of me. But I cannot have you going back to the village and crying Wolf to whomever strikes your fancy. I told you that, yet you betray me."

Alfred could hear the sneer in the Wolf King's voice.

"What's worse, you fool, is that you betrayed me to impress this girl. And you have doomed you both."

Alfred swallowed. In his arms he felt Martina tense with a growing anger.

"Did you lie to her, to get her to come out here with you?" said the voice in the blackness. "Are you in love with her?"

Alfred felt sick. Of course he could not say he loved her, not out loud.

"Answer the question, boy," growled the Wolf King. "Are you in love with her?"

Alfred swallowed a choke, and his voice came out strangled. "No," he said. "She convinced me to take her. She's just some girl from Latin class."

Martina was surprised to realize that she was hurt. She shrugged free of Alfred's arms, and spoke coldly. "I should have known better than to go into the forest with the son of the Boy Who Cried Wolf."

The forest held its breath, the wolves were still. The night cold poured in to replace the loss of Martina's warmth, and Alfred stood deserted in the dark with his loneliness and his lies, shame surging hot in his throat. Martina stood defiant and angry.

Finally, the Wolf King spoke, his voice strange in the dark. "Listen to me," he said. "The wolves gather. I have called to them by moonlight, by the howl of vengeance I have summoned them. From the deepest reaches of the black forest they are coming. I am building an army. I will rend and bite with a thousand teeth. For I have enemies. When the day comes, be sure you are not one of them. Now get out of my sight."

And the forest was empty again, silent except for the pounding of Alfred's heart and the low lament of wind in the trees. Alfred reached out for Martina in the dark, but she swatted his hand away and started back without speaking.

Alfred ran after her, hopeless. "Martina!" he called.

"I'm not fooled," hissed Martina. Her beautiful eyes were cruel. "I know you're in love with me. And you almost got us killed. Well, I'll tell you, I don't love you back. You're a liar."

Rifle And Sword

ALFRED STOOD IN VON KLIGGE'S OFFICE, his jacket torn once again and his nose bleeding from his narrow escape from the Tormentors outside. He was gaunt from his sorrows, but he had a plan.

Von Kligge observed him with unconcealed disgust.

"Why do you bother me again?" he growled.

Alfred tried to look confident. "I know something, Captain."

"What could you possibly know?"

"There is a man in the forest."

Von Kligge stood, a darkness in his face. "What?"

Alfred watched Von Kligge closely. He thought perhaps his plan was working. "He calls himself the Wolf King and the wolves do his bidding. He is coming, sir. He is building an army."

Von Kligge glowered. "It is in your nature to lie. Are you lying?"

"I am not a liar," Alfred lied, "nor do I lie now, sir."

"How do you know?"

"I have seen him. I have crept out at night and I have spoken with him."

Von Kligge felt a weakness in his knees but did not show it. He straightened his uniform and sat back down as if this was minor news.

At night on the wall for twenty years he had watched the forest, and knew every rustle of every branch, every flap of a raven wing in the muffled dark, and he had sensed even without knowing that something new, something dire, was now afoot in the brambles. He had heard strange howls in the wood, and the forest these nights was frozen as if it was holding its breath.

And a deeper part of himself knew more than that. He knew—he recognized—the howls in the forest somehow. In some part of his dreams he had heard those howls before. And, even though he was a soldier, he shuddered, for he knew also that the beast in the forest was coming for him.

"Prove it," said Von Kligge, a hoarseness in his voice.

Alfred could not, but he saw somewhere in Von Kligge that his words had taken some kind of effect. He gambled. "I am not a liar, sir. Give me a chance. I have told you something valuable, and shown you that I am committed and brave. Let me have a rifle and a sword. Let me walk the wall. Let me kill the Wolf King."

Von Kligge stared at the skinny boy before him. "Very well," he said, finally. "We will need every man we have."

Stand With Steel

ALFRED STOOD ON THE WALL in his brand-new uniform. It felt different to wear it from what he had expected. He had imagined that he would feel handsome in it, but he felt more than handsome. He felt deadly.

"I am a soldier of the wall," he thought. "I am a man. I have enemies. I have purpose. I am a rifle, and I am a sword." He stood rigid like a soldier should, his shoulders back, his chest forward, his heels together. In his hands he gripped the cold steel of his rifle. At his belt hung his sabre in its scabbard. He spent every night sharpening the blade, and now it was as razor-thin as his heart.

But in the depths of his soldier's soul, he had other eyes, which stared behind him over the rooftops and chimneys. They stared at a window, and through that window was Martina. Perhaps she was watching him too. Perhaps she was admiring his uniform, the way he held his rifle exactly the way a soldier is supposed to hold his rifle, a perfect silhouette in the dying sun over the forest. Perhaps she had forgiven him.

"What do I care if she forgives me or not?" he thought. "She's just some girl from Latin class. I am a soldier of the wall, and I care only about war."

The forest lay sprawled below him in a new way. It was neither frightening nor magical. It had become a system of battle-coordinates and firing zones. His eyes swept the shadows with mechanical precision.

In the distance he sensed movement, and in a wink his rifle was at his shoulder and his finger on the trigger. He peered down the barrel and in his sights was nothing but a crow on a tree branch.

He fired anyway. The rifle bucked and the crow spun in a puff of feathers to the ground.

Alfred did not blink as he levered the spent cartridge out of the chamber. There was a clink of brass, the casing landing by his boot. He was, to everyone's surprise, the best shot in the entire youth guard. On his sleeve was the crimson badge of the Marksman Corps, and on his shoulder were the two stripes of a corporal.

Raus appeared at the top of the ladder behind him. Alfred sensed him but did not turn.

"Your shift's done. I'm taking over," said Raus.

Alfred did not respond. Raus turned red.

"Listen, if you think I'm going to say 'Private Raus reporting' and all that, you can forget it. You're still Alfred to me even with your fancy stripes. Still little Alfred with his mouth full of snow."

Alfred clenched his teeth as Raus crept up behind him. "I heard about your little jaunt in the forest with Martina," Raus whispered, evil. "I guess you were talking pretty big, weren't you? The wolves are your buddies and all. But when they actually showed up you were crying you were so scared."

Alfred stared at the forest, his face hot. He fingered his rifle menacingly. But Raus continued.

"I'd stay away from Martina, if I were you. She doesn't like you much. You know who I think she likes?"

And Alfred's sword was out. Snarling, he swung, but Raus staggered slipping in the snow and the blade whistled past his still grinning face. The sword clanged off the battlement stone with a spray of snow, and Alfred, now off-balance, turned to see Raus drawing his own blade.

Alfred leapt, his weapon lashing like a snap-back twig, and Raus met the swing with a parry that shook the bones in Alfred's wrist. The hilts tangled, the boys turned and thrashed, metal screeching on metal. With a grunt, a hiss, and a wrench, they were free. Alfred slipped his blade slither-scraping along Raus's blade and twisted, yanked, and the sword came whirling from Raus's snatching grip to clatter-bounce off the scaffolding and land in the snow far below. Alfred snorted with surprise and delight.

With a roar Raus charged. His hand locked on Alfred's sword-arm, his shoulder hitting Alfred's chest with a wallop and a whoosh, his arm snaking around Alfred's neck, his hand clutching at his face as they toppled.

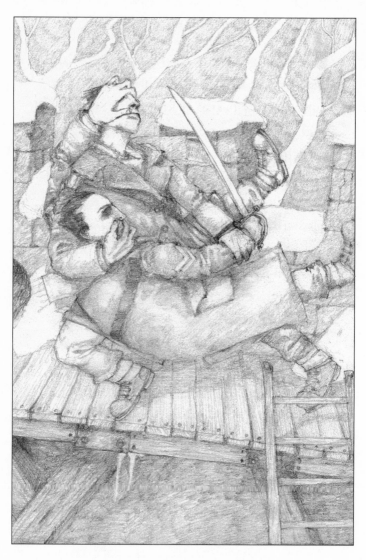

With a roar Raus charged.

They landed with a hollow whump on the wooden planks, Raus on top, his fingers spidering over Alfred's eyes. A knee in Alfred's belly, and he felt his sword slip from his grasp. They wrestled, fists and feet flailing, and Alfred felt his head slide over the edge of the scaffold, fingers like claws now around his throat. He struggled to breathe, his vision growing dark around the edges like a seeping shadow closing in.

And then: air, cool wind. Alfred shook his head, and there above him, Raus dangled in the grip of Captain Von Kligge.

"Enough," said the Captain. He dropped Raus, and Alfred scrambled to his feet.

Von Kligge stood between the two panting snow-dusted boys. His face was grim. A vein twitched in his forehead.

He turned to Raus. "Private Raus," he said, quietly, "if this happens again you will be whipped. Insubordination will not be tolerated."

Raus coughed and turned scarlet. Von

Kligge turned to Alfred. "Do you have anything to add, Corporal?"

"Yes sir," said Alfred. He looked at Raus with victory in his eyes. "Private, you are unfit for duty. You are dismissed. I will take your shift."

Raus clenched his fists. Von Kligge spoke. "Good."

The Captain turned on his heel and walked away.

"Fine by me," sneered Raus. "I haven't got anything to prove. I'm not the son of the Boy Who Cried Wolf."

Alfred watched Raus leave. Raus could say what he wanted. It didn't matter to him any more. As far as he was concerned, Von Kligge was his father now.

Raus

THE OLD MAN stroked his moustache thoughtfully. "Can you always tell a wolf when you see one, do you think?"

"Not so easily, I would say. A wolf can disguise himself. It is one of his talents," said the dog, who was lying on his back looking at the ceiling philosophically.

"Are you a wolf, disguised as a dog?"

"Once, maybe. But I've found life as a dog is much better than life as a wolf. I don't think I could go back. A wolf has no home, and I like our warm roof and a bit of stew in the evening."

"My days of wolf-slaying are done, at any rate," said the Old Man. "If I were still a soldier I would be more vigilant in my appraisal."

"The question is, are you a wolf?" The dog rolled over and peered at the Old Man suspiciously.

"I am not a wolf! How ridiculous."

"Wolves often disguise themselves as soldiers," said the dog.

"A wolf disguised as a soldier would be nervous indeed."

"Take Alfred, for instance," said the dog. "He is concealing something. He is clearly not at home in the world."

"Alfred is no wolf! Raus, maybe."

"No, not Raus. He is brutal but he is honest. He doesn't need to lie because he already has everything he wants. He is strong and well-liked."

"That is not much to want," said the Old Man.

"Nevertheless, he wants nothing he doesn't have."

"Except Martina," said the Old Man.

"That time will come," said the dog, and the Old Man shuddered.

"I think we should be afraid," he said.

"Indeed," said the dog. "We must do something."

"There is Evil in the forest," said Von Kligge.

Cry Wolf

ALFRED STOOD AT ATTENTION at the head of his platoon, the Honour and Eyes banner fluttering in the breeze behind him. On all sides the military might of the village was arrayed in rank and file, and before them stood Captain Von Kligge, resplendent in his gold epaulettes and holding his sabre upraised.

"There is Evil in the forest," said Von Kligge. "It is our privilege as honourable men to defend what is right and just, to do our duty. What is that duty?"

The soldiers shouted in unison. "To Stand with Steel, Captain!"

"Excellent. The entire safety of the people depends on you, the vigilant watchers. Our howitzers, our gattlings, our rifles, our swords, all are nothing if we are not warned. We will walk the walls with eyes wide open at all times. What will we do when the enemy appears?"

A deafening cheer: "Cry Wolf!"

Captain Von Kligge clicked his heels and saluted with his sabre to his forehead. "To your posts, men!"

There was a rumble of boots on stone like thunder as the soldiers scrambled to man the guns and the wall. Alfred could barely contain his excitement, to be part of a machine so perfect in its deadliness. He took his position on the wall with an almost unbearable pride.

It was then that he saw Martina approaching. How beautiful, the expression she wore of concern. He straightened his coat, and stiffened his spine, so that he would look exactly the way a soldier is supposed to look, a perfect defender, a heroic slayer of monsters. He turned his head to look out at the wood, but watched her nearing out of the corner of his eye.

But she did not come to him. She went to Raus.

Alfred's heart turned to stone as he watched, cursing the eyes in his head. Martina touched Raus on his cheek with tears in her eyes. She said something that Alfred could not hear, and Raus smiled bravely.

From within Alfred came a twisted, heretical desire: to cry Wolf at that very moment, to have the village turn their eyes and see that betrayal of his love. To show his power. To name Raus Wolf.

His lungs filled with it, and his throat

opened, but at the last moment he swallowed the word, which buried itself in his heart. And suddenly he hated his uniform and his weapons, he hated the wall, he hated the village, he hated Raus, and most of all, he hated Martina.

"I shall be a wolf, then," he thought. "If that is what I must be."

In the clatter of men taking their positions nobody noticed as Marksman Corporal of the Honour and Eyes slipped away from his post.

The Wolf Horde

ALFRED RAN THROUGH the forest, howling. His collar was torn where he had ripped off the insignia, and his face was haggard.

The wolf horde howled with him as he staggered into their broiling midst. They knew him now. He did not fear them.

The Wolf King sat in a throne of brambles in the middle of the field. He watched silently as Alfred knelt before him.

"I have chosen," said Alfred. "I am a wolf."
He listened, head bowed, for the Wolf King's
response.

"A wolf cannot be weak," said the Wolf
King, finally. "Have you forsaken that girl?"

Alfred raised his head. "She means nothing
to me," he said.

"Then you shall be my lieutenant. You shall
be my weapon."

The Wolf King placed his hand on Alfred's
trembling shoulder.

"Ten thousand thousand years ago, there
were wolves and there were humans and they
were the same animals," said the Wolf King.
"They hunted the same beasts on the same
savannas and the same forests. They drooled for
the same meat and their teeth were dipped in
the same blood. Their lungs heaved the same
winds and their eyes squinted across the same
world; they knew everything, then. In an
instant they knew the angle of every green leaf

on every tree, sensed the twists of the roots in the wet earth, the mice and the rabbits in their warm burrows. The birds arced through the crystal sky according to a web of paths that flashed in our brains with perfect clarity. The world was not a stranger to us, we wolves and we humans.

"But the humans of old longed for comfort, for warm beds with happy little fires and a nice stew in a pot. They dreamt of loving each other, and came to fear the terrible truth of the world. That truth is teeth and love is a lie. That beast and man face their deaths alone.

"So men built walls to keep out their own true selves. And from that day, man has made war on beast. Those who hide hate those who roam. Those who lie hate those who know. Because they are tormented by their own natures, and betrayed by their own dreams.

"The humans have guns and machines. They are only waiting for the day that their weapons will be terrible enough to exterminate all that runs free and true. We will not allow that day of sorrow to come. We have gathered an army. The final battle lies before us. We will begin with the village. No wall-dweller shall survive."

He turned away from Alfred, and addressed the gathered wolves.

"The victory of our race is at hand, oh, wolves. We have gathered. The packs are joined. Too long have we run alone from the guns of the wall-dwellers. Too many bullets, and not enough teeth. But now we are one horde with one purpose. Snarl of ColdBrook, do your troops pledge allegiance?" An old grey wolf with one eye barked and howled, and a cohort of wolves from the part of the forest called ColdBrook in the wolfish tongue howled with him.

"LongTooth of GnarlRoots! BlackTongue of ForestRim! RaggedEar of BurnedOaks!" One

"No wall-dweller shall survive."

by one the wolf generals thrust their heads into the air and merged their voices with the great howling. The forest trembled with the sound. Alfred watched, his chest tight with excitement.

The Wolf King bid Alfred to stand.

"You have a mission for the cause. You will return to the wall, and you will take your post. You must be the only guard at that place: Be sure there are no others. The horde will attack there. And you will stay silent. Now go. You will be honoured in the coming kingdom."

Alfred nodded gravely.

On The Third
They Came

ALFRED STOOD ONCE AGAIN on the wall. In the dark no-one could see that his insignia were gone. The moon rose slowly over the trees, and the wind blew cold over the battlements.

He heard a creak behind him, and he turned, his hand on his sword. There stood an old man with one leg, hunched on his crutch. Beside him was a frail and ancient dog. The Old Man had a look of great sorrow in his face.

"I would like to speak with you, Alfred, if you'll allow it," said the Old Man.

"Speak, if you must," said Alfred, his fingers slippery on his sword handle. He glanced nervously out at the wood. The forest was still.

The Old Man grunted as he drew closer. He leaned himself against the stone and spoke.

"I think you have seen a man in the wood. Is what I have heard true?"

Alfred stayed silent.

"He is your father. Did you know this?"

Alfred glared with hostile pride, for indeed he had come to know it in his bones. "Say what you have to say, and quickly, old man. I am on guard."

The Old Man looked at his dog, his forehead wrinkled with concern. The dog looked back encouragingly.

"Very well," said the Old Man. "I will tell you something perhaps you don't know.

"Your father once stood on this very wall

and watched this very same forest. He was in love with your mother, desperately in love with her. And then one day he saw her with Von Kligge, who was then a handsome young corporal. And what did he do? He cried Wolf. Do you know why he cried Wolf, Alfred?"

Alfred did not answer. He shifted impatiently. He thought he saw a shadow move in the forest, but it was only a raven.

"There were two reasons," said the Old Man. "The first was simple: He did not want them to be walking together, and the only thing in his power to do was to sound the alarm for an attack, so that Von Kligge would have to run to take his position on the wall. But the second reason was this: He wanted them to know he had seen them, that he knew he was being betrayed. That to him, they were wolves.

"It happened twice, of course. And the third time he was not lying. But as we know, nobody believes a liar, even if he is telling the truth.

"He escaped into the forest. I know because I helped him, for he was my son."

Alfred frowned at his grandfather. The wind rustled the aged fellow's thin white hair, and for a moment Alfred felt a strange pain in his chest that he did not quite understand. His fingers loosened on his sword-hilt.

"He is better off in the forest, I think," said Alfred.

Alfred's grandfather sighed. "He's not better off in the forest. He was terrified to go, but we both knew it was his only choice. He was just a boy, and when I snuck him out through the hole in the wall, it pained me to see him so scared. But I could see already that he was beginning to harden, to hate those who sought to punish him, to hate the village, to hate Von Kligge, even to hate your mother. A soldier should not hate, Alfred. A soldier ought to protect. He must love those he protects and protect those he loves. And he should never lie."

Out of the corner of his eye Alfred saw the glint of eyes in the forest. His father was coming. His father was the King of Wolves. The King of Wolves was no liar. The Old Man could say what he wanted but he didn't know the truth.

"I wonder," said Alfred. "Was my father lying when he cried Wolf? Or was he calling for them? Three times he summoned them, and on the third they came."

The Old Man looked with horror upon his grandson.

"Begone, Grandfather," said Alfred. "I have a duty to fulfill, and I cannot be distracted."

The War Between
Beast And Man

WITH GRIM PRIDE, Alfred saw the eyes gathering in the shadows. Slowly the numbers grew, pair by pair, as the great legion amassed for attack. He glanced from side to side along the wall—no other guard was in sight. Only Alfred could see the gathering in the forest. His father trusted him, and it made him feel like a giant.

Soon every shadow had its gaze, and the trees quivered with the wolfish breathing. The wind was warmed by ten thousand lungs. The vengeance of the wolfish was near, and Alfred grinned. Never again would he suffer at the hands of foul Raus. Never again would he be called a liar. He would be called Prince of Wolves, and his wrath would be mighty and merciless. He would live in the forest with his mother and father and the wolves would obey and Martina would bow before him.

He would scorn her nonetheless. She was the liar, not him, and he would never forgive her for it. He would never forgive anything ever again. A wolf does not forgive. A wolf takes what he wants and destroys when he pleases. Alfred could not wait for the attack to come.

Suddenly, he heard a giggle. His reverie broke, and his eyes snapped into focus. There, in the forest below him, he saw Martina. She was walking with Raus. They were holding hands. And behind them were the eyes.

Alfred growled low in his throat and his

belly churned with hatred. The cursed Raus would ruin everything. Alfred raised his rifle, and sighted along the barrel. He could do it.

He squinted down the terrible line of the bullet's passage, and his finger trembled on the trigger. Raus was in plain view. The button on his coat glinted. Easy shot.

And then out of the forest came his father. He swept from the shadows with silent speed astride his wolf, his sabre raised, in a single leap, the wolf's paws outstretched, arcing through the air with perfect precision. The sword blade flickered through the air, flashing down, a whisper in the night. Raus's face frozen in mid-grin, his hand extended in a gesture for some joke. Martina laughing. Their arms entwined. The sword slicing the eddying fog.

The edge of that sword was vengeance, for all the tears of Alfred's life. It was punishment, for all the moments Martina spent with Raus and not with Alfred. It was retribution and it was justice.

But Alfred loved Martina.

His gun bucked. The report sounded far away. A burst of hot smoke from the barrel. A piece of lead screamed through the air.

The blade twisted from its path and the Wolf King crumpled. His head turned in a contortion of surprise, and his eyes, glowing, pierced Alfred's own for an awful moment. The wolf reared and spun and the Wolf King toppled from its back with a silent slow backwards fall, his body landing on the earth to lay sprawled amongst the tangled roots of the forest floor.

Martina and Raus looked up at the wall, knowing nothing except that a shot had been fired, but Alfred was already gone.

Behind them, the wolves silently retreated. Pair by pair the eyes disappeared, and slowly the wolf horde returned to the forest deeps. Their king was dead. The war was over.

The Boy Who
Cried Wolf

ALFRED THREW THE WRETCHED RIFLE
to the ground and ran from the wall. He
ran without sense, choking on his breath, stumbling, staggering. Around him the village slept
its ignorant sleep.

He found himself at the door to his house,
and panting, he pushed his way through and
closed it tight against the dire night and the
horrible thing he had done. He tore his coat
from his shoulders, buttons clattering down

the hall, and ascended the stairs to his mother's bedroom. His scabbard clanked against his calves as he climbed. A weariness overwhelmed him.

His mother was awake. The room flickered with the candle lit by her bed. Alfred slumped to the floor before her.

"Mother," he said, his voice hoarse, "I have shot my father."

Eva feared her son had gone mad. She gathered his haggard face in her hands and held him to her. "Alfred," she whispered. "All is well. Whatever you have done."

Alfred squeezed his eyes shut and quietly shuddered in his mother's arms. She rocked him gently for a long while, and in that embrace he slowly slipped away from the world into sleep, through the secret passage that leads to the realm of dreams.

In his dream he stood in the snow, which fluttered down flickering in the moonlight, gathering on his shoulders. The wind was soft and cold.

He stood on the wall. The entire village was asleep. He listened to their breathing, and watched their breath turning to steam and rising through the chimneys to be caught in the wind in little clouds that swirled around him. He found he could reach out his mittened hand and touch the wisps as they drifted by on their way into the forest. He watched them pour over the wall and into the shadows.

He saw the breath fog moving through the trees, ragged clouds that loped and panted, and he realized the night was full of wolves. For a moment he was terrified, but then he remembered that the wolves were only made of the breath of the sleeping village. With each snore, each rising chest, a new beast was formed to roam in the night.

He opened his mouth and shouted a shout with no sound. "Wolf," he cried, and he felt the wall shift beneath his feet. The ancient stones began to crumble. "Wolf," he cried again, and the gates groaned on their hinges, the towers leaned and creaked. "Wolf," he cried once more, and the wall gently fell into dust. He floated down to the ground and landed on his feet.

The village was in the forest once again like it was in time before time. And the clouds of breath returned to their slumbering owners. In his dream, Alfred smiled.

He did not hear the creak on the stairs, or the heavy footfalls in the hall. Eva stiffened. "Somebody's there, Alfred. Who's there?"

The dream collapsed. Alfred wrenched himself from his slumber, blinking. He was in his mother's room.

He heard a ragged breathing in the shadowed hall and drew his sword. "Show yourself," he cried, but the sword trembled in his grip.

A voice came from the darkness. "You have deserted your post, Alfred."

There stood his father.

Into the room his father slumped. His face was pale, and his beard thick with sweat. He held himself up by the doorframe. In his coat was a singed hole, and around his feet gathered a black pool of blood. He bared his teeth in a strained grimace that might have been a grin.

"I would have made you a prince," he said. "And someday you would have been king. I know who you are. But I suppose I should have known not to trust the son of the Boy Who Cried Wolf."

Alfred swallowed with fear. In his father's hand was a sword, its iron point dragging on the floor. The knuckles of his hand were white.

"Erich." His mother spoke.

"Ah, Eva," said his father. "I hoped to see you again. It has been a long while."

"I did not know you were still alive." Alfred heard a strange tremor in her voice.

"I am."

The Wolf King breathed hoarsely and

stared with hollow eyes which glowed nonetheless like the moon through the tangled trees. He was very tired. And he spoke.

"I love you, Eva. Will you come away with me?"

Alfred saw his mother's eyes and they were dry and hot. The room was silent for a long moment. "No."

The Wolf King snarled, his face contorted. His fist tightened around the sword handle, and he drew himself with a harsh breath to his full height. He towered, a bleeding beast, his eyes crazed. "I am the King of Wolves. The forest is mine. As far as the eye can see there are trees and beasts and they all bow to me. A king is offering you his heart, Eva. You cannot refuse it." His gaze was murderous.

It was pride that made him murderous, but pride is made of hope. The candlelight illuminated his shaggy face, and he looked upon the gentle comfort of the bedroom, the covers of the bed askew, the warm furrow in the pillow left by the head of the woman he had loved so long. He thought of his life, a thousand nights curled in his gnarled bed of roots with the cold wind blowing through the silhouetted branches that were his only roof, how he clenched his teeth to keep them from shuddering. And he gazed upon his poor terrified son, and his one true love, and realized that his hardened cheek was wet with a single cold tear that slowly trickled from his hollow eye into his beard.

Eva looked at him without pity. "Your heart is yours to do with as you please, as is mine," she whispered.

The Wolf King felt his fingers twitch and the blade fell from his hand to the floor with a clang. With a soft groan he felt the pain in his belly and the blood in his boots. For a moment, he smiled at his family, and then slipped back into the darkness of the hall.

Alfred and Eva listened to the halting tread

of his boots on the stairs and then the door creaking as it opened. Alfred ran to the window and looked out into the street.

There stood his father, stooped, the snow beginning to fall on his hair. He winced as he straightened his back and then slowly his mouth opened and his neck arched. He stood frozen like that for a moment, and then a single cry came from his throat, a cry of grief not war, a cry of a boy not a beast.

"Wolf!" he shouted with all his might, and the call flew through the village, through the doors and windows, into the forest and to the winter clouds above.

A shot broke the air and the Wolf King fell. On the wall, Friedrich Von Kligge lowered the smoking barrel of his gun.

A Wanderer
Of The World

THE VILLAGE CELEBRATED the final fate
of the Boy Who Cried Wolf. "His punishment was much delayed but much deserved,"
they all agreed. Captain Von Kligge was awarded the Wreath of Ash for the second time, and
the ceremony was raucous and joyful. Eva did
not attend.

Alfred did not visit anyone before he left.
Martina never knew what really happened on
that night, how Alfred had saved her from the

sword of his father. She thought of him occasionally as the years went by, but did not mention it to her husband Raus. One day she told the story to their daughter, but she told it as a fairy tale, not as the story of her own life.

Alfred, for his part, lived long. He saw many wondrous things in his travels, and never returned to the village of his birth. One day, in a city on the other side of the sea, he met a woman who had never seen a wolf. They loved each other until the end of their days.

THE END